Sol

A Hun

Nathan Isbourne

For Peace

As long as we remember them
There's always still a chance,
The war supposed to end all wars
Will still become a fact.

As long as we maintain their graves,
Rub fingers on their names,
We may one day all realise
The price of peace was long since paid.

*In memory of Harry Patch,
and dedicated to those who came home, to
those who didn't, and to those who stand
guard till today.*

Oh how lovely men have been, how utterly indispensable, so wonderfully dependable. They heard my whimpers and my sighs and turned them into battle cries; they heard the pleas of Common Sense, ignored the cost of Recompense. Oh how willing men have been to wash their hands of decency, wish harm on fellow human beings, and stand up for Supremacy.

- *War*

I gain no greater happiness, than to see the smile upon the face, the hand held out from a different race, to be embraced by a different faith, the many tones of many skins, that stop their days to call me friend.

- *Brotherhood*

Glory to the victor! Glory to the victor! But Wellington chose his words quite well, was accurate in what he had to tell, that no darker sentiments are ever felt, than the melancholy of a battle won, the dreadfulness of victory, and I will never disagree.

- *Glory*

Thankful I have been, and thankful I will be, when leaders choose to legalise the killing of good men. I'm happy when a madman strikes another down, I'm happy when a lover loses self-control, but the happiest I have ever been and the happiest I could be, is when leaders raise great armies to conquer other lands. But remember Time records all deeds and the consequences that occur, and when you look through the index pages you'll find no other name but mine, and in war, I don't even need to hide.

- *Murder*

I would not need to stand my ground, I would not need to shout you down, I would not need to scare you off or rattle feebled bones, if all agreed that pointing guns will only lead to error, if all agreed that helping hands would put an end to terror.

- *Defiance*

I bow my head to those, who've shown bravery over fear. I doff my hat to selfless souls, who've put other's lives before their own. But even so I shiver, when seeing brave men die, for needless reasons and senseless treasons, before Man thinks of peace.

- *Courage*

I do not exaggerate, I do not lie, when I talk of my own value: I'm precious and I'm priceless and should be treated so. Take care to guard me safely, take care to hold me tight, once doubted and once faded, I'm hard to be restored.

- *Trust*

I'm easily recognisable, I'm easily underlined, when looking though the history books of Man's committed crimes, but look around the present and gaze into the future, and you will find to your surprise, I'm a master of disguise.

- *Insanity*

Though at the head of the table, though placed before the rest, though given highest status and considered among the best, when discussion turns to argument and argument to blame, when tempers flare and fists are clenched you'll often find my voice is lost beneath the squabbling furor, you'll often find my chair's removed, and I'm pushed outside the door.

- *Forgiveness*

I raise my head whenever I can, I dash your hopes and thwart your plans, and once I've got inside your brain, rest assured I'll build my nest, rest assured I'll do my best, to control the outcome of your thoughts, pull down your wavering spirit, subdue morale, remove the fight from in your heart, turn victory into running legs.

- *Futility*

I am the mindset of success, I am the chisel of cutting edge, I am the loophole when all seems lost, I am the builder of willingness. I turn the tide when it's boring down, I step across the visible line, I pull Hope back up onto its feet, I wear the grin of an optimist.

- *Audacity*

Prologue

Soldier Tom lives both in this world and in the beyond, yet is as real and tangible as anything you can touch with your hand or feel within your heart. He is timeless and imparts the wisdom he has gained and the lessons he has learnt through millennia of wars and countless, bloody battlefields. Here, he raises his voice with a great pride in his beloved nation, with a great love for its people – and indeed all people - and with the greatest of hopes for its future. He is an entity of peace caught up in the quagmire of Man's ambitions, selfishness and greed. He talks to each and every one of us.

Through scenes of the First World War and scenes of Remembrance, Soldier Tom highlights two things: Man's seemingly insatiable appetite for war, yet his huge capacity for peace. He describes Man's rightful desire to live in peace and his right not to pick up arms, yet he poignantly depicts the struggle within the mind when one has no choice but to do so, and shows the horrors that await when one does and also when one doesn't. Soldier Tom, fights because he must. Soldier Tom risks his life because he must, and Soldier Tom kills because he must. But, he deeply questions the reasons behind this 'must' and just like Harry Patch he profoundly objects.

This is a poem, not a historical document. One can easily tear great holes in the chronology of events, in the varying use of first and third person singular, of the past and present tenses, even find that two voices speak instead of one though only one hand holds the pen. Yet, despite these deficiencies in consistency, it has been written: written with a great desire for peace; written with a patriotism that unites people, not divides them; and written in the hope that all readers, whatever their backgrounds, will be uplifted to be able to maintain and demand peaceful and unselfish ways. This is especially incumbent on the elected leaders of the world. The voice of Soldier Tom speaks out loudly towards them and, like Kitchener, the finger of Soldier Tom points out directly at them.

The poem may not dispute the reality of war, but it is still a sincere and earnest plea for peace. It holds nothing back to describe the foolishness, idiocy and pure, intransigent stupidity of war, and the underlying unnecessariness of war. It is especially poignant that it is written now, on the one hundredth anniversary of the end of the Great War: a war Soldier Tom believes still can be the war to end all wars.

- *Peace, for November 11th 2018*

Soldier Tom

I am Soldier Tom,
Long since dead yet still alive,
Long since gone yet still around,
Not of the living, yet far from dead,
Not of the breathing, yet full of breath.

My voice has stayed reluctant
Far too many years,
But now I can't be silent,
I'm full of pressing thoughts.
I must untie my stifled tongue,
Unclasp its reticence,
And use the soul that I've been given
To carry on the fight for peace.

Though my last breaths left me long ago
I'll use the breath that I've been given
To find my voice again,
The voice that was bereft of air
As I bled on battlefields,
And raise it to a higher pitch
To tell of things that I have seen,
Of things that I have learnt,
To talk of life and talk of death,
To talk of war and peace,

Of things that I remember,
Recall with great dismay,
Of things both past and present,
Of things that I can see.

I've turned away when asked
To recount my glory days,
My exploits fine and bold, they say,
That deserve renown and praise.
These I've gladly hidden,
Preferring to forget,
With a mouth full of denial,
With sweets between my teeth,
With grandchildren on my knees
To stave off moodiness,
Ignoring the futility,
Cold shouldering the mess,
To prevent the gravitation down,
Distressed at younger minds,
Eager for adventure, racing off for War,
Oblivious to its wretchedness,
Ignorant of its gore.

Though heroes I have known and seen
And courage oft displayed,
I'll never make a call to arms,
For I have lost too many friends,
For I have seen the bloody guts
And I have heard the screams
That still remain intact as fact,
That still adhere in memory,
That even now until this day

Still surface in my dreams,
That cause my troubled mind
To doubt the reasoning.

I've lived and died in many wars,
Been carried off with awful scars,
And seen myself ten thousand times
In the burning city,
In the fields of blood,
Sitting down exhausted
In a corner out of sight,
A man with head held in his hands
Trying to make sense
Of what cannot be understood,
Grieving to have witnessed
What men can do to men,
Not knowing if he was blessed or cursed
To come back in one piece,
With a head full of ungodly noise,
With flashbacks full of dreadfulness,
With Hell almost a certainty
And Paradise certainly lost.

He may be six foot two and over fifteen stone,
He may be full of British phlegm,
Have a stiffened upper lip,
But still I see the tears run through
The dust upon his jerking face,
Feeling even more alone
With more mates laid to rest.
But in this man I see no weakness,
His tears bring back his strength,

His sense of duty is profound,
Will bring him to his feet
To carry on the fighting
Until the job's complete.
Like all strong stoic working men
He'll get on with the job,
The job that's plain and simple
To return a state of peace.

I've learnt that War is heartless,
For it doesn't have a heart,
It's just a name we give to what
Men will do on Earth.
It's not a part of creation,
It's not a form of nature,
It's just the outcome and a mirror
Of Man's weakness and failures,
Of ambitions and misjudgements,
Deficiencies and egos,
Bewildering intransigence
And diplomatic blunders.

War is like a sickness,
Yet Man contains the virus
And contagion smites whoever,
It even ails the peaceful.
It feeds on men's resentment,
Quadruples human scorn,
There's always plenty to be had,
Its stomach never rumbles:
And even saints are not immune
To deadly falls and tumbles.

It despises men with open arms,
An olive branch's for burning,
Show it a crack in coexistence
And you're already invaded.
Your humility and your tolerance
Are weaknesses it curses,
Turn your backs to run,
It delights in hopeless cases.
Better to fight with sticks and stones
Than gift it with your land and houses,
A greed for blood uplifts it,
Makes slaughter even easier,
A lust for pain inspires it,
And revenge tastes even sweeter.

It is disease for sure,
But belligerents hide the cure
Despite the doctors, and the scientists -
Who've sometimes helped it rather well -
It lives on fear, it lives on hate,
Devouring all it can.
It's latent in the human heart,
It plans within the human mind,
It'll only be outwitted
By a foe who is unwavering,
It'll only be defeated
By a will that is unending.
Yes, it's latent in the human heart,
But so again is Peace.

*****

There was a time, millennia back,
As a man brought up to never covet,
To never steal or take a life,
When I was caught in Dilemma's clutch
And had to face and ask myself
How far would my pacifism bend,
How far would it stretch
Before I thought to raise my hand,
To brace myself, to clench my fist?

How long should I let the wolf
Draw closer with each day,
That only wants to feed on flesh
While baying at the gate?
Do I let it in and greet it with a smile,
Expect it to accept my peaceful will
For endless peaceful ways
While it consumes my wife and child,
To kill at will with a will to kill,
Look on as if it can't be true,
Appalled my arguments aren't received,
My intentions ignored or ridiculed,
Expect the wolf to think like me
When all it wants is an easy meal,
To sink its teeth in healthy meat,
Quench its thirst on wholesome blood,
Fulfill the logic of its need?

Should I stay at home
Behind the garden gate
And thank the able soldier,
A stranger yet a friend,

Who chose before I ever did
To risk his life, to meet the fight
Far earlier than I would,
Who kept me and my family safe,
Contented in our bliss?

Yes, my pacifism was quite easy
With a soldier standing guard,
Was quietly convenient
Though the wolf was still at large,
And I, gratefully forgetful,
Protected in my yard.
But when would I lift up my arm,
When would I join the fight,
When would I venture out, prepared,
To leave my comfort zone?
When would I understand the need
To soldier on and carry arms,
Though a pacifist still at heart,
To defend my land and home,
To accept the unbearable practicality
That peace, sometimes, only lies
On the other side of protracted hell?

In no-man's-land I stood
Not knowing where to turn,
In peace I had security,
In war I'm glory bound,
In peace I'd gain a ripe old age
With children round my feet,
But War would carve my name upon a stone
For all eternity.

In peace I have my lover's arms
To hold me through the night,
In war, honour pulls so strongly
At my ardent heart.
In peace all things are common sense,
But I am young and not yet wise,
And in war my spirits effervesce,
Are righteous for a cause
And the bugle's call does so arouse,
Lifts up my dallying soul,
Entrances me to pledge the oath
To Country and to Sovereign,
To defend the Crown and Nation
With Dignity and Honesty,
And despite the fears and warnings
Of all of those with age,
Despite the hopes of all the years,
I duly march in step to fight,
Not thinking, just like other men,
That I would have to kill,
That I would probably die.

*****

And years rolled by, they could not stop,
Just as the sun at dawn,
Countries' borders were to be erased,
Willy-nilly to be redrawn,
And the greatest of all wars
Had finally arrived,
The tyrant wished to take the land
He'd dribbled over for so long,
The bear was restless, yawning,
Its hibernation over,
It stirred and growled a fatal mood,
It could not be ignored.

And as always I have learnt,
It is always just the same,
A tyrant will not stop,
He only has one mind.
He only serves himself,
The rally call of his desire
For greater power, for others' lands,
Spurred on by lack of peaceful sense
At all and any price,
Indifferent to the cost
In human life and human pain,
Urged on by lust for blood,
A deluded historic role,
And a people who know no better
Than the propaganda that they're fed.

His aircraft, guns and armies
Amassed along his borders,
He'd made allies with whoever

Cowered to his orders,
While those at home remained ill at ease,
Ill-prepared in disbelief,
Unwilling, as is right,
To fight as dogs of war,
Unwilling, as is right,
To shed their carefree lives.
But fight we should, or lose our land,
Hear stomping feet on British streets,
See another's flag replace our own
Upon our ancient upright poles.

So when the finger pointed
My mind was set to go,
I would not let my people be
Oppressed and trodden down,
And would not let its children
Be schooled in foreign lies.
And though I did not know the outcomes,
And though I did object,
The consensus of our dreads and fears
Was unfortunately 'I must'.
So my avowed intent became
To be a soldier boy
Until a lasting peace was found
And the bear had lost its claws.

I signed upon the dotted line,
Took the shilling from the sergeant's hand,
Was patted soundly on the back,
Pledged loyalty to my land.

I was born the nation's child,
Was schooled the nation's ways,
Was raised on fertile British soil,
When the call to arms was made.

I volunteered, I walked on up,
The line grew long behind me,
I entered in my Sunday best
Then marched in uniform.

I did not ask what I would do
For love gave me all worth,
I did not ask what fate would bring
For duty bore me forth.

I gave the shilling to my wife
For bread and milk and cheer,
My mother couldn't see me off,
But dad shook hands between his tears.

Then the whistle blew,
Then the train pulled out
And while the brass band played
And the flags were waved
I settled on a wooden bench,
A young Englishman off to war.

*****

War appeared far sooner
Than we had ever thought,
Me and Jack and Bill and Bert
Who'd sat upon the other bench,
Now leaning on the troop ship rail.

A ball of flame filled up the sky,
Made lanterns of the other ships,
Defined the long horizon,
Put sunset back into the night.
The deathly boom came later,
It echoed from chalk cliffs,
Dampened by the distance
It rolled and coiled across the surf.

Later on the debris
And some bodies washed ashore,
Tides brought home their native boys,
Who'd drifted to a deeper height,
Partially clothed, partially burnt -
Those not locked in iron chambers
Between bulkheads of stagnating air,
Between bows and beams of iron,
That sank abruptly to the bed -
Bloated, half buried bulges
On the fresh-washed shores,
Cleansed and cured in North Sea brine,
Salt rubbed in our sores.

She was lifted by a direct hit,
Her hull ripped open wide,
She listed then she vanished

While coasting to the north.
The hunter fired tubes one and two,
Stalking, counting, waiting,
Brooding in the silent deep
Until the shockwave shook them.
Then all was joy and cheering,
They were smitten with their kill,
Victory recorded in their log:
A column for the tonnage,
But nothing for the dead,
Counting lucky the moonlit night,
The outlined silhouette,
And the trail of billowing engine smoke
That pinpointed the death.

How obscene to put the quest
Above a human life,
How mad, how sick the mind becomes,
When War pulls all the strings.
But it was all so beautiful:
The fiery, reddened sky,
So admirable the technology,
The design and stealthy power,
Well worth the patient pursuing,
The fanfare and the medals:
Brave no doubt, and heroes,
Lurking in the deep,
But jubilant and willing killers
Of their fellow Man.

And when our feet touched land again
I'm sure I heard the voice of that

Which lay beneath the foreign soil,
Forlornly and ironically warning,
Of sweat and tears, of blood and toil, it said:
Marching still, after all these years
Towards the pestle that awaits,
Lockstep feet above my head,
Unaware, the blood soaked fields beneath
Where many undiscovered lie
Heaped upon each other,
Covered by the dirt.

Pounding soles and jolly songs,
Eager hearts, like mine, of old,
Adventuring into action,
Danger their mistress,
Plunging into loss, distress and bitterness,
Pushing on through wind and rain
Over decomposed remains,
Volunteers maintaining freedoms,
Of loved ones back at home,
Soldiers upholding foreign policies,
The interests of a few.

Can you hear me call,
Trampled under heavy boots?
Unfelt, our ghostly arms grasp up
To stop your ardent stride.
It's true, I once was young
And once was glad to fight,
Once blinkered, seeing all but foresight,
But now I'm very old
And try to stay your feet,

Yet lie unheard
With those whose midnight hour
Chimed in their early morn,
The chorus of the dawn of wisdom
Not yet even heard.

Don't you feel the sadness, in the grainy soil
Where Anger first unleashed itself,
First took a life, gave Murder birth
With healthy lungs
That shouted out to justify
A gross, unwholesome, gruesome act
Where Man revealed his real self,
Unveiled the violence in his core,
Misfortune sown beneath his pores,
That breeds such ill in such excess,
Gives rise to shame and great distress?

Don't you feel the moist field weep
Where Anger first provoked, aroused,
Inspired Slaughter to shout the battle cry,
Run amok with dreadful thirst
To spray out blood and spread out gut,
A date long lost to History,
A horror plot where humans screamed,
A story plot where minds explored
The many ways to please a lust,
To splatter offal,
And the extent to which we're apt to hate?

Don't you feel the country tremble
Where Anger first contrived, conspired,

Convinced Ideology to divide all unity,
To think it ruled and had the right
To quash discord and reason,
To draw its lines uncivilly
Across which Truth now dared not step,
To make all bow, all toe the line,
To silently acquiesce,
Where freedoms disappeared
While the State insisted it be revered?

Don't you feel our only Earth quake
Where Anger first expanded schemes
To place all life in jeopardy,
Took Stupidity and made it wish
To take a breathing, vibrant world,
And obliterate, incinerate,
Totally eradicate,
Deny humanity of its inheritance,
Deprive the world of its existence,
Discard all good and great achievements
As if Man never was? It said.

But we carried on a whistling
And the voice didn't linger long,
It seemed to know the futility
In uttering its words.
It seemed to know what lay ahead,
The way from life to death,
The ways of youth and ignorance,
The path to gain one's wreath.

*****

On we walked in single file,
Ammunition trucks raced by,
A purping horn cacophony,
As bigger guns arrived.
Ahead I saw a soldier
Who'd lost his kit and rifle,
Then I saw the soldier
Had also lost his face.
He meandered to the left and right,
Then fell into the ditch,
Clutching at a photograph
Of his wife, his staff, his strength.
But things were so chaotic,
No able man could aid him,
But at least he had his sense of balance,
Could get back on his feet,
He stood a while then raised his hands,
Felt sunshine from the south,
Then climbed back on the gravel track
And knew which way was west.
Our orders were to march,
Not stop for anything,
So, I was grateful when I saw him helped
By a corporal on a crutch,
And then by a sergeant regular
Who'd been deafened by the shells.

*****

When morning came I was assigned
My first task of the war,
It was something I had never dreamt of,

A shocking, gruesome chore.
I was to pick up pieces
Of the blast the day before,
But my sandbag did not carry sand,
But arms and feet and more.

And when I thought this task was finished
A woman called me over,
Beckoned me into her life
With French I did not know.

She pointed to the window sill
Where a hand lay still and burnt,
Then over to the clothes line
To a forearm soaked in dew.

Her gestures led me to believe
She thought a bird had hit the window,
A thump accompanied a little crack
While she was kneading dough.

But when I picked it up
I felt metal next to skin
And rubbed away the hardened blood
To find a wedding ring.

My heart stopped for a second,
My breath was held inside,
I continued rubbing till it shone
As if caressing my own bride,
Hoping she would never hear
The news this man's wife would,

That although the ring was still intact
His body was no more.

The woman kept on talking,
She appreciated my help,
So I thanked her and I wished her well,
And put the hand into the bag
While she washed away the smudge.

And then the roar began,
A barrage of intent,
Manmade lightning filled the skies,
Industrial thunder filled our ears.
A continuous bombardment
For three days and three nights
Of those souls within the other's lines
Deeply burrowed in their holes,
Praying deeply to our common Lord.

And my thoughts went back to Liz,
As they hourly did,
The girl I married very young
In the village church,
The lovely girl I left at home,
The loving mother of my boys,
And I talked to her as usual,
Though parted by two shores.

Hold on to me my darling,
Hug the kids for me,
In the morning there's a push,
God willing I'll see the evening,

But the chances aren't so good
For Jerry's well-positioned,
His guns deserve respect,
But we're still to strike him hard,
To hit him where it hurts.

I saw you in a dream last night
That gladdened me and took my mind
Far away from war,
Now I can run up to his guns
With only thoughts for you.
I do not fear the battle,
My mind's no longer here,
I'm standing by your caring side,
Smiling cheerfully,
Looking in your darling eyes
And that is all I'll see
With each step forward that I take
Until the dusk is here.

But if this be the day I die,
With God I have no qualm,
For He has done His very best
Through peaceful men and peaceful means
To keep the world from harm.
It's purely men who are to blame,
Who've set the wheels in motion,
With undeveloped hearts,
With errant wants of gain,
It's truly men who are at shame,
They've set the course of this foul day,
Who'll put me in my grave.

And looking to my left,
And looking to my right,
New faces filled our trenches,
Thousands upon thousands,
Not just only white, not just only Brits,
The Commonwealth joined forces,
The black, the brown, the fair, the swarthy
Hindus, Muslims, Buddhists,
Africans and Indians, Burmese, Nepalese,
Along with more familiar faces,
Other allies that arrived,
Had come to join the fight.

Yes, other races, other colours,
Other religions too,
Untrained in and ill-equipped
For this modern war,
Shivering in their tunics, hardly given time
To acquaint themselves with the cold and damp
Before going over the top
For Britain and for Harry,
Dutifully following orders,
Maintaining discipline,
Mostly out of honour,
But mostly
Never to return.

Then when the barrage stopped
And the smoke shells had been dropped
We could hardly hear
As the ringing in our ears kept on,
And just to make sure Jerry knew,

The bloody whistles blew,
And up and over the top we went,
We were on our way.
We climbed and ran into the white,
Into whatever hell was there,
Men heading for the devil's lair,
Men whispering our Father who art in Heaven,
Who the chaplain said was watching over,
But God was looking down unable
To do little or even nothing
To halt the chaos and commotion,
The frenzy of destruction.

*****

As aristocracy obliged,
The Lieutenant was first to climb,
And he was first to drop,
Looking back to wave us on,
Pistol high, held in his hand,
A lucky shot into the dark,
Then Agincourt repeated:
Men funnelled into narrow bands
Of sodden land,
Culloden gaily transmuted,
Running into overwhelming guns.

I didn't know who he was,
The second to fall that day,
But I'm sure it wasn't how he wished to go,
Inconceivable a year ago
After given so much training,
Hardship and live drills,
Given our equipment and so much heavy kit,
The voyage on the ship,
First time abroad,
But not the sights he wished to see,
To slip before he even saw a Fritz.

He splashed about a bit,
Legs clasped by indifferent mud
Until it clung just tight enough
To pull him down into the mire,
To keep him still and underneath,
Trapped until his breath gave out,
And final bubbles burst then stopped
Upon the surface of the murk

To show the ingenuity of Death,
The irony of War,
To take a man into their breasts
By unforeseen collusions,
Of untold foolishness,
Of wisdom not yet learnt,
But at least the telegram showed sympathy,
'Killed in action' it simply said,
Which was far more comforting and eulogising
Than unnecessary facts.

His body was found when the rain had drained,
He'd given his life like all the rest
Amidst the unrecognizable fields
Of Mons and Passchendaele and the Somme,
Of Marne and Picardy and Verdun,
Of a list of flattened towns and cities,
Of carnage along the Western Front.

And then the smoke got thinner,
It drifted in the wind,
We ran on with our bayonets fixed
Searching for loop holes
In the tangled, barbed defences
That proved all too adept and able
At tangling men as well.

And then the air was clear
And Jerry was still there,
They'd dug in far more deeply
Than the generals had explained,
And Jerry's eyes were keen,

Their rifles were well-aimed,
And men began to dance and scream,
Maimed by burning shrapnel,
Machine gunned down in droves,
First Bob then Jack then George,
Good soldiers gone in seconds,
Running to their firing squad
Though no crime was committed.

But still we took the trench,
The handful of us left,
And waited for reinforcements,
But they never came,
So we were ordered to retreat
And give the trench right back,
Walking passed the wasted dead,
Through the scene of untold death,
Through those who'd only captured
A piece of no-man's-land,
But at least what lay beneath their bodies
Truly belonged to them.

*****

And all this time, the Press was there,
But he did not write all that he saw,
Farther still from what he thought
And far from what was printed,
Far from what the folks would read,
A melange of partial truths:

From behind the lens, I followed them,
The line of round tin hats,
Hunched along the shallow trench
Moving forward, bayonets fixed,
Urged on by their sense of duty,
And a tot of rum,
Their only body armour,
The pictures of loved ones
Tucked inside their inner pockets,
The letters kept from home,
Read a hundred times,
Kissed a hundred more.

One by one they clambered up,
One by one they disappeared
Into the silence of the smoke,
Unbroken human chains
Moving on with quickening pace,
Their names unknown,
Their accents thick,
Until all hell broke out,
The hell they knew awaited them,
Continuous rounds of rifle shot,
Machine guns and grenades
Through which they had to make their way

To capture back a few more yards
Of unearthly, broken soil:
I counted them all out, he thought,
But he counted only four come back.

The shock contorted features
Upon his disbelieving face:
He couldn't show his pictures,
He couldn't write his piece,
He couldn't let the truth be known
For victories sold his papers,
And as far as leaders were concerned
Morale was paramount.

*****

With time we learnt to laugh,
God, the way we changed,
Ridiculous guffaws,
Hysterical releases
To skirt past deep black holes
That sucked some into suicide.
Laughter at the rats and lice,
The tragedy and sewage,
At the way the hapless died,
The poor sod with his trousers down
Filling the latrine
Who literally didn't see it coming,
But could hear its whistle growing.

We were laughing, we were joking,
Telling anecdotes as reverie

To remove us from this morbid land,
Away from fear, from gross disgust,
To keep our minds towards what's sane
While insanity ruled in Victory's name.

I wrote home every day
Eager like the rest
For any word of folks and friends,
To read of love maintained.
Cheery, always filled
With camaraderie and bravado,
Nothing slipped between the lines,
No awful truths, no dreadful scenes,
I always wrote that I was fine,
Talked of mates and stripes on arms,
Of joyful paddling in the mud,
Deckchairs made from wooden crates,
No hint of tripping over skulls
Nor mention of exploding shells.

But Christmas came and went,
The Times grew broader with its lists,
And neighbours' sobs were quite distinct,
Yet nothing slipped between her lips,
Just bedtime stories for the kids
Who knew not what war meant or brought,
Her fears were kept behind her smile,
Her tears shed while alone in bed.

Her heart stopped when the postman
Walked up the garden path,
Not knowing if his hand, this time,

Would bring my familiar scrawl
Or a message from the King.
The war was taking toll
Of planes and ships and men,
But also took its quota
Of broken hearts back home.

God, I hate all war,
I loathe, detest, abhor all war,
I rue the day I signed my name,
Regret the day I joined the Game,
But still,
I've found no greater love
Than for the men beside me
Who share my lot, my daily bread,
Who I would gladly die for.

And that was life and death
For months, then years to come
Each assault, each retreat, each push, each pull,
I turned into a different man,
Who testifies to youth long gone
In such short a space of time,
Of innocence lost and paradise gone,
Of callouses on calloused hearts,
Of ruptures in benevolent thoughts,
Of pity rapped in military courts.

*****

The weather was another beast,
Unhelpful to say the least,
Apart from sheets of rain,
Mists rolled in to hide the day
Gave opportunity to creep on up,
But heavy feet were a telling sign,
Crunching boots on a frosty morn,
Sent bullets aimed at unseen steps,
Then more were aimed at injured moans,
Till men fell into enemy trenches
Or, having lost their way,
Fell back into their own
And were kicked back up at rifle point,
Or shot dead then or at tomorrow's dawn.

Yet even so humanity
Was given leave to tend to those
Left gravely injured and immobile
Between the sorties, even if briefly,
When shells stop falling and bullets flying,
When sounds continued to haunt the living,
The sound of severed arms and legs arose,
The sound of blood-filled lungs composed
The symphony of bravery,
The melody of audacity,
And the encore of great tragedy.

Humanity returned and took its turn
To climb on up and wander through
The heaps of flesh, the awfulness,
Wonder aghast at all the mess,
Guided by each salient note,

Drawn towards each gargling discord
To find the faces stretched and drawn,
Faultless horror expressed in pain,
And chaplains finished lives cut short,
Medics bandaged jagged bones,
Stretcher bearers carried wounds.

They acted fast for time was running,
Visiting hour was quickly closing,
Each casualty ticked, each loss recorded,
Added to the colossal butchery,
The inventory of misadventures
And catalogue of malefactions,
The archive of misanthropy
And life consuming treachery.

But even humanity retreats when ordered,
Slips back down behind the parapets,
Disappears like fading dusk
As War is there to recommence,
Head strong and single-minded,
It continues strong, hail and hearty,
Revelling in the hideous party.

God, the fool I was,
God, my naivety,
To have to put aside my peaceful ways,
To pick up gun and learn to fire,
To push my bayonet in the guts
Of someone I had never met,
To live with devils who relish gore,
The dogs of war who would be thugs

Outside the army's given role,
Who live psychotic dreams,
Who wake each day already smelling
The blood they're urged to spill.

God, how much I hate this fight,
To see my humble brothers run
Into the sights of rattling guns,
To watch the brave and duty bound
Fall head long into squelching earth,
To gain a trench of rats and lice,
With another just a hundred yards behind.
God, close my eyes, take me away
So I no longer see,
But if I live until the end,
Please, take away my memory.

Some men are impaled by war,
Live nightmares in their beds,
While others find euphoria
In firing guns and exploding heads.
Some men dream of peace and calm,
Wish Heaven down on Earth,
While others never really feel alive
Unless shaking hands with Death.

And therein lies the rub,
The thrill and call of War,
The adventure and unknown,
The elixir of the rash,
That promises all too much.

It's counterfeit and ill-advised,
Yet even so it trumps
Common sense and often law,
And always ends by sending
Hapless thousands to their graves.

*****

There was a boy I knew,
Arrived the day before,
To see his face
Was to hear his scream,
To see his eyes
Was to know his fear,
Young man marching on to pipes and drums,
Killed outright by fright and guns,
Romance and glory, delusions gone,
Illusions shed,
He died before his death had come,
His heart beat stopped in rigid form,
Body froze before the frost,
His breath was taken before the blow,
Enticed into the lion's pen,
A boy thrown in the reaper's den,
A rigid statue carved by lies,
An effigy of horror cries.
Don't talk to me of duty,
Don't speak of sacrifice,
Don't point the patriotic finger,
Don't try to justify:
Ours *is* to reason why,
Ours *is not* to do and die,
Ours *is not* to pick up guns,
Ours *is not* to shoot and kill.

But we do, 'we must', we say,
But must 'we must' I say?
Yet soldier on I will
For I am Soldier Tom,
For I was there and then I wasn't,

I was neither here nor there,
But I surely do assure you
I was and am both there and here
And viewed and view all things, and
God, how I hate all war,
But fight I will if 'must' must be fulfilled,
If 'must' must be believed
And mustard gas released.

And that was on the ground,
Was only one dimension,
For War will gladly utilise
What's below us in the tunnels
And above us in the heavens.

The fight was fair, no rules were broken,
Though the Scourge had made the field uneven,
He'd had his kill, had survived three weeks,
He'd pursued and bitten the dragon's tail,
Now the dragon was gnarling back.
I watched them high above my head,
Rolling left, then rolling right,
He climbed then dove,
Banked again and looked around
Still in the enemy sights,
Couldn't shake the bugger off,
No clouds in which to hide or peel away.
He heard the machine guns' ratatatat
Above the rushing wind,
The ricochet of bullets against the engine block,
The interrupted roar, the loss in power,
Another ratatat of red hot metal

Pierced the fuel pipe, started the fire,
Turned cockpit into fiery Hell.
The ground beneath his destination now,
As fast as could,
But hasty air took hold the flames,
Wrapped them round his leather,
Too long he fought to gain control,
Height became his newest foe,
Would deal the killer blow.
The flames were burning to his skin,
He smelt the smell of his own death,
No wish to jump, no parachute,
He'd go down captain of his ship,
Though willed the aircraft to explode,
His hands no longer any use,
He used his knee to push the stick,
Heroics to inspire all kids,
To dive into the ground:
He didn't wish to enter Heaven
Along a trail of smoke and screams, but did.
He hoped they'd understand
On the resurrection of this falling man
That evened up the tally -
Two killed meant two more losses
To the family of the world.

And concerning what I mentioned,
For a moment I felt fear, then shame and guilt,
An inescapable position,
Self-preservation, who'd be quicker,
Bayonets aimed at each other's guts,
His against mine, thrusting hardened steel,

His eyes, like mine, growing wider,
Whiter with each step,
Youth, adventure, duty, folly,
Pretty maidens with white feathers
To kick you out the nest,
Ineluctably, War brought me to this point,
To keep my life, but diminish my humanity,
To keep my humanity, but lose my life.

But for that moment all was fear
And reaction to the fear,
A lad, just like myself, a little blonder,
Same height and build,
Under other circumstances a welcome friend,
Who became a constant companion
In that thrust and twist,
The blade up behind his ribs,
Blood pouring from his lips.
Until this day he visits,
Though a 'good' soldier shouldn't think,
But this one does, still wakes in sweat,
Wakes the neighbours, angered and belittled,
Helpless to control events,
Shocked at what this death had meant,
The legacy of another war.

This was the point where all
Illusion disappeared,
When needs must, and 'must' be mustered
And authority's pointing finger
Pointed out from every wall.
A hero brave they said,

But 'nay' I said, and 'nay' again,
He was neither friend nor foe,
But is a constant reminder,
Of the sharpened point of life and death
Where humanity imploded,
And now I find it is my turn
To point out my own finger.

After years of contemplation,
Overriding everything felt,
It's anger I now feel
When I see the glare within your eyes,
And repugnance fills my innards
As I see you run towards our lines,
But not for you my friend,
Though perhaps you wished me dead and gone,
For the ones who put the prejudice
Deep within your soul,
For the ones who instilled hatred,
Who taught malevolence,
Who convinced you I'm less human
To be tortured, maimed and killed.
So here you are my friend,
A violent, surging mass,
No need to follow orders
You raced before the rest,
But one thing they didn't tell you,
I 'will' defend my land,
I do not turn and run away,
For I am Soldier Tom.

Today I used my bayonet
To lance your acrid heart,
And tomorrow I'll place a bullet
Right between your eyes,
So here's some honest words my friend
To make you think again,
Words to make you ponder
To carry to your grave:

Do you fully understand
That the blood that spills from me
Will fertilise and energise
Our dear and precious soil,
Will give it strength and turn it fierce,
Turn daffodil and primrose
To heather and to thistle,
Turn Labradors to psychopaths,
Make murderers of gentlemen?
And though I may be driven down,
Smote onto my knees,
My tongue be severed, my chest be pierced,
There waits another British man
And behind him yet another still
Made taller, stronger, fiercer,
More eager than before
To defend our home,
To keep our forests, fields and hills,
To disperse your brains along our coasts,
Beat you back to sulk a while
While maggots feast upon your corpse
And make you wish you hadn't felt
The urge to steal our land.

But here's another truth
More pertinent than the first,
I wish you peace, I call for peace,
For the 'truth' that you'll soon see,
That when the war is done,
When all the tears have flowed,
When all the blood is shed,
When all the graves are filled,
When all unnecessary gore
Has fulfilled the ambitions of a few,
When all the smoke has cleared
And all prejudice that was instilled
Has been removed,
I will kneel to pull you up,
To put you on your feet,
And though you may still fear
And find it hard to trust,
I'll place my eyes in line with yours,
The eyes that never lie,
And you will clearly see and know
That my brother you had always been,
That my brother you are still.

*****

But for all of those who died
In the agony of it all,
Happy he will be,
And envy's what I feel,
If he can talk as this one does,
For he found peace denied to me
Once he went from Earth
With acceptance and clear sight:

Do not worry ma,
I'm not alone, I have my friends,
The roar has stopped, it's quiet here
And peace begins, if not down there.
Yes, I was young and I was fast,
But the bullet faster still,
It caught me from the side
And pushed my soul out from my breast,
It took me quick, I felt no pain,
Was laid to rest before I hit the ground -
I was running through the mud,
Then strolling into fields of green
Like those at home that I loved best.

So, do not shed a tear too long,
Though I know you will,
At least my body will return to you,
Wasn't blasted into hell.
I'll visit you in thoughts and signs,
And you can bring me flowers,
While many others wonder,
Where their sons may be.
Yes, it was hell, but only short

And what I saw I will not tell,
But went I did, with no desire
To take a life, unless I must,
Knowing well that I could die
On the first day or the last.
So, do not worry ma, I'm happy to be here,
Knowing you are well and free,
To be British still.

So, do not worry ma,
You'll get the letter in the morning,
But I am fine,
You'll see my smiling face
All nice and clean,
All spick and span,
Standing by the side of you,
My hand upon your flowing hair,
My lips upon your forehead.
I am at peace, I am at rest,
Out of the stinking, wretched cold,
Among a merry bunch,
Among the laughter of my mates,
Sipping at an Ansell's,
Eating fish and chips.

You see my soul has gone,
But I'm not really dead,
And I did my bit
In the uniform that I loved,
And you will see me often ma
Walking round the house,
You won't be left alone ma,

For I will be about,
You'll see me come and see me go,
You'll see me for a second or two in full view
On the other side of a blink.

*****

We had a three day pass,
Were wearying to a station,
Were hidden movements in the night,
That took us through what once was Ypres
Where new faces heading forward
Met old ones heading back,
Where hobnails scratching cobbles
Met rotting leather tied to feet.

Columns shied from tremendous flames,
Entrancing, raging cauldrons,
A city misshaped by cannon and planes,
Infernos reflected in startled eyes,
Structures fast becoming ruins,
Cracking, collapsing, crashing,
Burying streets under piles of rubble,
Adding to the pit of muddle.

Necks craning up at toppling walls,
Met sagging shoulders with heads bowed low,
Soldiers heading for their deaths
Met those escaping with their lives,
Aghast and inward marching up,
Haggard and outward trudging back,
Glowing clean towards the trenches,

Muddied matt towards rest stations,
Through the appalling stench of burning horses,
Pyramids of animal corpses,
Carcasses falling into beds of ashes,
The young men suddenly not so eager,
Young men quickly growing older,
Who'd soon be numbering far, far fewer.

I saw myself again,
My questions left unanswered,
Too weary or too kind to tell
What lay ahead, what lay behind
Our deadened eyes, our hollowed stares
That only those returning
Could bear witness to,
Would begrudgingly expound,
Would reluctantly recall.

I called in to see our Charlie
Who had two fingers shot away,
Two digits from his right hand,
The index and the middle.

He'd winced and cursed and hopped about,
Had lost his trigger finger,
But perhaps it was a binding contract
Not to wag two fingers.

Even so he didn't want
To take the boat straight home,
He'd too found that greater love
For the few mates still around.

He ceased to be a rifleman,
Put his gun back in the rail,
He ceased to aim his bullets,
Became a messenger instead.

I recalled my first day's task,
Was thankful for my luck,
My wedding ring was still attached,
My Liz was still my spouse,
But though War hadn't ripped my body up,
It had ripped out part of me,
If I returned I wouldn't be
The man she fell in love with.

I looked around the hall of beds,
A nurse began to do her rounds,
Her apron rustled against her frock,
Starched white rubbing on starched white,
Clean and crisp, just like the linen,
Stepping lightly in-between
The coughing and the fitful dreams,
The hissing lantern gently lighting
The faces of those who slept,
Of those who couldn't sleep,
Of those whose whispers
Sometimes made her smile,
Stop to whisper back,
Sit upright on a young lad's bed,
But mostly brought a disapproving frown
And short-lived laughter followed
By a soldier's snore
Whilst horizon's distant guns continued

Rumbling into war-numbed ears,
Cast lightning through the restless night,
Threw silhouettes on whitewashed walls
Like flickering bulbs about to blow,
And like food upon a well-stocked shelf,
Each empty bed refilled.

I watched another soldier
His eyes looked far away,
The nurses smiled and turned his sheets,
Refuting what he knew.
He'd seen the doctor's shaking head
In the corner of the ward,
He'd seen them lifting others
On stretchers with covered heads,
He'd heard the telling groans and sighs
In the beds across from his,
The final gasps of men's last breaths,
Their final grasps at life.

His hands were white,
His veins were thin,
His pulse was weak and slow,
The frame told him his legs had gone,
If no-one told him so.
The pain told him his end was near,
Though morphine did its best,
Yet he didn't ask for parson,
For pastor, vicar or priest,
And though he didn't wish to die,
He'd long since made his peace
When he didn't think to question,

When he didn't hesitate,
When a duty he fulfilled and bore,
Till the day he lay in silence listening
For the Roll-Call with his name.

He'd heard the call, he said farewell,
Went merrily down the street to war,
With shining buttons, with grinning mien,
To cheering crowds, to waving flags.
He left to glory and to pomp,
To drums and pipes,
Enthralled, imbued, aroused,
Returned within a shroud,
With two medals on his chest.

Within a coffin, within a hearse,
Within his town, the soldier lay
Without the life that he'd been given,
Without ears to hear the horses' hooves,
His unit's marching feet,
The parson's deep felt eulogy,
Rifle shots above his grave,
The bugle's final call.

Without eyes to see the grief,
Proud townsfolk at every vantage point,
His family without speech,
Stooped before their boy,
Too deeply saddened to say mere words,
Tears falling on the dug up earth,
His mother fell upon the box,
The headstone stood engraved and stark.

But I have to ask which view is better?
Pride we have and pride we show,
But pride will not end war,
It comes before a fall,
But sadness could and broken hearts,
For these things don't inspire
The continuance of strife,
These things should be listened to,
Countermanding pride.

*****

We thought it was a stalemate,
That neither side would bend,
For what better way to balance power
Than wars that never end,
But Churchill's tanks arrived
Along with willing Yanks,
Well-equipped and now quite ready
To shoulder sacrifice.
And then we whispered victory,
And then we spoke aloud,
My God it could all finish soon,
We could imagine going home.

The word came not long after
That the war would stop at eleven,
But the bullets and the shells
Kept flying overhead.
How many more were killed
In the final hours and minutes
I do not know, I cannot say,
As stockpiles of munitions
Were unstocked and thrown away
Across the enemy lines,
But I do know the deafening roar then stopped,
Stopped on either side.

There was a moment's hesitance,
A nagging disbelief,
And the question, 'Was it really true?'
Still passed between our lips.
Then a German officer
Stood up above his trench,

By habit we could have shot him,
But thankfully no-one did.
He doffed his helmet and bowed our way,
Bestowing honour on the victor
With relief in his eyes that it was over,
That he would hold his children,
That his children still had a father,
Then turned and marched his men away
And we saw he wasn't the real enemy,
The enemy was War.

Yes, it really was all over,
There was instant joy and cheers,
And our minds returned to better things:
Of what we'd soon be doing,
Of what some planned to do,
To the thought of seeing home again
We'd denied ourselves before,
All avidly filled our hearts and minds,
Returned to being real.

But though the war was over
Our wars continued still
As insistent recollections
That pushed and shoved and spoilt the day
That begged the other question,
Was it worth the while,
What we'd all been through?
And the merriment diminished,
Became small talk and exhaustion,
And all we wished was a place to rest,
To close our eyes and sleep,

To forget what we had seen,
And sadness at the friends we'd lost,
And the uncertainty of our future,
Not knowing that the powers that be
Would soon meet at Versailles,
That in league with one another
They'd assure another war.

It's true I got a medal
Made of ancient iron,
But it wasn't on my mind
As I ran between their cannon,
In fact I begged my legs for speed
As hundreds fell in front of me,
To the left and to the right,
Behind me, all around.
Yet it was I who got the medal,
A general pinned it on,
But although he pinned it on my chest
And others showed their thanks and pride
I didn't give the most I could,
I didn't give my life,
I didn't pay the highest price,
I didn't get my name inscribed
Upon a simple cross.
To them belongs the victory,
To them we owe our freedom,
To them we bow our heads each year,
For them the day is stopped.

Although I have the medal
The honour lies elsewhere:

I do not wear dark glasses
Hiding two deep hollow holes,
I do not have two crutches
Replacing severed legs,
I do not suffer shell shock
As much as others do,
I did not take my own life
As others did when seeing
More than they could bear,
And, this time, I'm not decomposing
Under a battlefield.
I only have a piece of metal
Showing far less sacrifice,
To me of far less value
Than giving up one's life.

Yes, it really was all over,
But was it worth the while?
For there never is a winner,
Just those who kill
More than the other,
Who shed their blood
A little less,
Cry tears incalculable
Like all the rest,
Whose streets and cities are destroyed,
Where neighbourhoods pick up the pieces
Of the buildings and the dead,
Counting sons and daughters
Taken from their hearths,
Tragically departed,
Ruing the day the whole thing started.

And though the vanquished nations
Are burdened down with shame,
The victorious ones should share the blame
For perpetuating the circumstances
Of gross mistrust and hate,
For failing to maintain
A lasting state of peace.

And then return to Blighty,
On the troop ship rail alone,
Never had a gentler breeze
Brushed across my face,
Nor a milder summer sun
Made garlands out of clouds,
Of perfect white on perfect blue,
And never had the air been filled
With such pleasant English smells
Of fresh cut grass,
Of barley, hops and corn,
As I came home and stepped ashore
Looking for a face
No longer drawn with worry,
For War had also left its marks
Across the skin,
In so many hearts,
Of those at home
As well as across the fields
Of foreign lands,
The unlucky ones we left behind
That soaked my joy
When I should have been happy
To be alive,

But instead continued living
With the dead,
With grief
And guilt at brothers gone,
Though none should be within my head.

I scanned among the shifting crowd
Until I finally found
A smile that'd never been so full of love,
Of love and tenderness,
And eyes so never full of tears,
Arms never before so far outstretched,
And when we finally touched and clasped
We stood embraced till the shudders ceased,
Renewing vows without a word,
And I kissed her lips and she kissed mine,
And I kissed each extra line
Across my Liz's face.

*****

*****

A great grandson came bleary eyed,
Walked into the kitchen,
Around the old man's feet he stood
Holding battered Teddy,
One hundred long years on
From when the Great War finished,
A hundred long years on
From when the roar diminished.

He looked up at Soldier Tom
Who looked down at the little tyke
And winked and hoped the little lad
Would never own his mind,
Would never have to 'must',
Would never go to war,
Would never know mistrust and fear
Or too early turn to dust.

The old man rinsed his teeth
And then he put them in,
Twirled his regulation brush
Upon the wetted soap,
And shaved above the kitchen sink,
His collar rolled to free his neck,
Looking in the tilted mirror
On the window ledge.
He wiped the misted glass,
The kettle had just boiled,
The morning dew grew lighter
As the day grew gradually brighter
And the townsfolk would be readying
To head down to the square.

And today the sun would also appear
To hear the 'last post' sound.

He sat upon the back door step
To give his shoes their shine
With the remaining bristles of his brush
He'd kept and used throughout the years,
And stroked the dog that muzzled
Up against his knee
Before it limped out to the yard
With dimmed white eyes
To sniff its patch half-heartedly,
To totter as it cocked its leg
To pee against the tree.

Upstairs, he took the old shoe box
From the bottom drawer,
Took out the ribboned medals
And his broken watch
That only told one time
Whatever time one looked.
He held them for a while
And thought of all his mates,
And wiped away a tear,
Then put the watch upon his wrist,
The medals on his chest,
And the poppy in the button hole
Of his November vest.

He closed the garden gate,
His head already high,
His sciatic foot well hidden,

Walking tall and proud
Towards The Anchor mustering point
To take his Legion place,
To show the others in the parade
What it meant to march in step
Upon command,
Upon the drummer's beat,
With shoulders back and swinging arms,
Eyes not flinching, straight ahead,
Things an old soldier never forgets
On the Day for Remembrance.

Standing at the memorial
While the nation stood in silence
He watched the crosses of the Flag
United with good reason.
He stood before the monument,
He stood before the names,
And stood before St. Andrew,
St. Patrick and St. David,
Knowing who they really were
And what they really meant.
But his mind fell on St. George,
The patron of his country,
And his mind caught on a train of thought
Explaining who George was:

Legend, yes, an imaginary myth,
Yet powerful he still is.
He was with our Harry,
He is in our hearts,
He was the body and the spirit

Of every man who fought.
He is Stan and Ben who tunneled
Beneath the enemy lines,
He's Fred and Bob who charged
Across a field of mines.
He's Bill and Bert who laid
On top of barbed wire coils,
And Wilf and Alf beside Jock and Taff
Who sang above the noise.

He's not the gleaming knight
Upon a handsome steed,
He's scarred and limps, he buckles and bleeds,
But only knows one way to go,
Towards the point where death is near,
Where every stride is a moving step
To bring us nearer peace.
He is those who do not hesitate,
Those who ignore fear,
For whom death is just a hazard
And a life is to be offered.

He's those who see a job,
A duty to be done,
Who live and die for others,
Always at the front.
He's also Maud and Mable
Who tended livid wounds,
He's Madge and May who took away
And washed the blooded sheets.
He's Edna and our Vera,
Our Dora and our Sall

Who smiled whenever they could,
Who held back tears and carried on,
Who held the hands of many
Before they left this world
.

He cares about the folks back home,
He's there to help the people,
He watches men give all they can
And then give even more.
He insists they be remembered,
Be honoured and live on,
He wishes all the nation
To know its greatest pride.

For Britain is the Giant Oak,
The Bulldog and the Pomp,
But then again a mountain
Whose darkest hours are precious veins
Within the rock of Equal Right,
Between the ore of Common Good,
Where crystals lie of noble deed
And gold dust shines to mark the dead.

Its soil is rich with sacrifice,
With bones compacted tight,
The names upon the granite slabs
Bear witness to the price.
Our debt is all too clear to see,
We work, we rest at peace,
Have freedom to believe and think,
Old enemies are now friends.

But we won't hear disloyalty
To the many and the few,
Their loss shall not be squandered
By rats beneath the pews.
And we will not stand bigotry
By those with differing views,
For they who gave their lives for us
Wore many different shoes,
For those who stood with us and Harry
Should always be called friends.

And I am Soldier Tom,
I don't believe in half mast,
To me the Flag stays high,
Like me stands tall and proud.
It never flops or mopes about
When the wind shifts to and fro,
It is the Flag within each man,
That doesn't bow or cower down,
That doesn't stoop or fester,
That doesn't bare its chest to show its scars,
Or wallow in self-pity:
It's made of stronger stuff,
Of British phlegm and grit,
And doesn't balk or back away
When the dirt's thrown at the fan,
But pushes to the forefront
To lead each other on.

It's the Banner of plurality,
The Standard of tolerance,
The Colours of a nation's promise,

An unwavering belief
In each man's global right to live his life
In peace, goodwill and freedom,
In each man's right to walk in safety
In the streets of Manchester or London.

So, I don't believe in half mast,
Don't lower the Flag for me,
Don't even give a quarter inch,
I'm not lowering myself you see.
I stand for coexistence
With those of peaceful ways,
And I live by peaceful means,
And follow paths of peace,
Free to hold my hand out
To place it in another's,
Not to raise it upwards
To strike another brother.

*****

So I can't remain in silence,
I cannot stifle thought,
For I am just one more
Who is the quiet voice,
Who asks someone to put the words
Upon a printed page,
Or say the words upon the Earthly stage,
Just as was done millennia thence
When the first pen tried to stop a war,
Reminded us of the pain it brings,
Of loss of blood and human life,
And in the end that no-one wins.

Tyrants come and tyrants go,
Bringing occupation and oppression,
Leaving those who wish to live in peace
To fight against their will,
Leaving wakes of horror cries
And furrows full of human flesh
While the Earth demands all wars to cease,
That 'we' may bring the end in sight,
That through remembrance
And through goodwill
The Great War may still be said to be
The war to end all wars,
And if not forgotten, and with lessons learnt,
The war to bring a lasting peace,
A peace that ends all war.

Yet even so, as the listening hand writes,
Puts cloaks upon otherworldly thoughts,
Plants sentiment upon a soul,

And tries to find the fittest words,
Its efforts pale when placed beside
The deeds of those within their graves.

The writer can only try his best
To tell what war's about
And hopes to move all hearts to peace
With parchment and with quill.

But the real author lies deep underground,
In silence wades through thick and thin,
His words are feet through splashing mud,
His sentences his marches lines,
He laughs before he clambers up
And fights until the very end.

His war is filled with verse,
His paragraphs his battles,
His chapters his campaigns,
His tomes the bells that toll,
His epitaph his epilogue,
His oeuvre the peace he brings.

What is it but poetry
That's carved in stone around the world,
In the names and ranks and regiments
Of soldiers neatly placed
In serried lines just as they stood?
So, in the end, when all is said and done,
This is the real poetry of war,
Not mine.

But, the arrow only flies
As far as the bow allows,
Its steel will only strike
The ones within its range,
Its barbs will only pierce
The armour that's too thin,
It is of little use
Before a wall of stone.

The pen that writes of peace
Will touch a peaceful heart,
The quill that's dipped in ink
Will work its best to bring
A merging of two worlds,
A preponderance of trust,
But is of little use when left unread
Beyond a wall of lies.

*****

Tom knew his time was short,
Even Remembrance took its toll.
With his medals back inside the box
And his head upon the pillow
The old man saw old friends arrive
To take him to their world.
Not sure if she were still awake
Or half into a dream
Liz saw Tom sit up on the bed
Before putting on his clothes.

Where are you off to, love,
More errands to be run?
Off to the allotment
Or to the Working Mens?
You turn and smile and blow a kiss,
You look so young and bright,
Are those the shoes you used to wear
When dancing through the night?
Your hair has lost its grey,
Is blowing in the wind,
Just like the time when we first met
Walking down the strand.

What is that you say my dear,
Are you talking in your sleep,
You'll see me in a while,
You're going to be a little late?
Your shirts are in the wardrobe
Washed and ironed like new,
Well wrap up warm and mind the step,
You know I always do.

Your grip is very strong my love,
The hand I've always held
When leaving every day behind,
And welcoming each dawn.
Your words are growing softer
As you talk within your sleep,
And your breath is even quieter,
Are you all right, my dear?

She held his hand while his final words
Were muttered incoherent,
And his final breath was stuttered,
Relinquishing his presence.
His fingers held on tighter
Unwilling to release
His hold on life, his hold on her,
And despite the indignities of his age
And the pains of higher years,
It was of greatest certainty
That their love had never ceased.

And then she fully woke
And saw she was alone
And laid her head upon his chest
For tears to flow across his breast,
While waiting hands reached down
To lift him from his limp remains,
To guide him back to higher life,
To the world beyond our own,
To flow back to the ocean
That holds all time and deeds.

Her farewell was a kiss
Upon his cooling brow
As gentle and as tender
As on their wedding day,
She lay beside him through the night
While in his deepest sleep
For the pact they made
When he came back
To never be apart,
Was a promise true and to be kept
Set solid in her heart,
And she closed her eyes until the dawn
And then she didn't wake,
For to be alone without him
Stopped her heart as well,
And this time it was Tom's hand
That pulled Liz up instead.

Their children didn't wish
To remember them as old,
So, although they would have disagreed
At the expense on bodies moulding,
They used the undertaker's skill
That gave the needed chance
To see them one more time
As they used to be to them,
The father and the mother,
The parents as they used to be
With death taken from their skin,
With apparent weighty flesh returned
To bones that had lately shown,

Restored to strength, to dignity,
Asleep except for breath,
With personality and character
Set across their faces,
Prepared with care for eyes that cared,
With other aged frailties
Shrouded under silk.

Gratefully they could see them thus,
Could touch them to express their love,
To wish them well and bon voyage
Though no longer were they there,
But taken with the passing wind
To their subsequent destination
And wondered what they themselves would say
When they in turn met them again,
When their own times here on Earth had gone,
When Time had turned its circle.

*****

Yes, a hundred years has gone
And even Happy Patch has finally passed.
We bow our heads and give our praise
To those who fought
And those who gave their lives,
Were blown to bits or boxed back home,
Who fertilise a foreign soil,
Who heard the call, who loved their land,
Who joined the Game, who fell

To Empire builders' falsities and claims.
Yet remembered they should always stay
And honoured they should always be,
But are they truly honoured,
Those who kept us free,
By policies and interests that require
The sending off of others
To kill and bleed and die?

What is the purpose of these rhymes,
The reason words were written,
Words describing Man's great quest for peace
Yet his appetite for war?
For sure there have been heroes,
For sure we owe a debt,
But war arrives through failings
And peace departs through selfishness.
For sure I always stop at Eleven,
Doff my hat to those in Heaven,
And for sure I kneel with all the nation
Before the Cenotaph.
But even so I remain attached
To dear old Harry Patch
And like he who saw it all and returned intact,
I gladly do object.

Yes, they will not be unattended,
The stones will not be lost,
The names will not get weathered
Of those who gave the most.

The grass shall not grow high,
The roots will not disrupt
The serried lines of fallen men
In the cemeteries of France.

For these the sun will never set
Though their eyes closed long ago,
For these the peaceful never rest
To keep their hope alive,
That men respect the rights of others,
Learn not to harbour grudge,
That men will fully understand
It's better not to judge.

Lie deep they do, and silently,
But their memory calls out loud,
It talks of selflessness and heroism,
Of sacrifice and pride,
But reminds us of the toll in lives,
The loss and grief and agonies,
The great unnecessariness
For which they paid the price
To one day lead the world to peace,
If regrettably and deplorably
A century too late.

As long as we remember them
There's always still a chance,
The war supposed to end all wars
Will still become a fact.

As long as we maintain their graves,
Rub fingers on their names,
We may one day all realise
The price of peace was long since paid.

As long as we let others keep
The lands that are their own
And do not deem to overlord
Their loss was not in vain.

As long as leaders talk of peace
And do not think deceit,
Recall the cost in blood and tears,
Then crops instead can fill the fields.

As long as foreign interest
Includes the interest of others,
There is no need to send in troops
To keep the rich in power.

As long as peace is bred in schools,
Respect for life maintained,
Another war will only spill
From the grossly unintelligent,
Deluded or insane.

*****

So, who am I? I'm Soldier Tom
And I will soldier on.
I'm in our nation's soil,
I'm in our nation's soul,
I stood beside Boudicca,
I fell at Harold's side,
I rose for Haig and Kitchener,
Suffered Singapore and Dunkirk,
Yet turned the tide at Alamein,
Before being thrown beside
A narrow Burmese trail.
I fought amongst the Many
Then fought among the Fewer,
And stand to even now,
As I always will.

I've fought and fought again,
And I'll fight again if needed,
I saw heroism amongst the danger
And kindness within the carnage,
But in my heart I wish for peace,
That hatred will be ended.

Yes, I am Soldier Tom,
Part of a great nation,
A nation of achievement,
But Empire's not included.
I was before and I am now
And I'll be present in the future,
Fighting if I have to,
But calling men to peace.

I thank you for your time,
For listening to an older soul
Whose thoughts may be contentious,
But still they're full of feeling,
Contain impelling meaning
That more lives won't be lost,
That more lives won't be squandered,
That names won't be forgotten,
That the war to end all wars
May still restore to all men
The long relinquished Eden.

Yes, I am Soldier Tom,
I've passed yet still remain,
I live in Time which mirrors time,
Time that folds and folds again.
I live in ebbs and flows
Of laughter and of tears,
And wax and wane in deep regret
With friends who gave the most one could
Standing tall and proud.

But God, how many more to die,
How many more, how many more,
How many more to die
Before we reach our senses,
Before we fill the trenches,
The abysses which keep us all apart,
That perpetuate the fighting?

After millennia years and more
Of my particular lives,

Closeted in the world of Earth,
Watching from beyond,
Immersed in untold wisdoms
And the immensity of thought,
How often I have seen
The breath of Life and Peace
Suffocated by War and Death,
And the gentleness of Man
Subsumed by pitilessness.

I fear what lies ahead,
For those I leave behind,
Fear that all is naught and naught is all,
That Earth could end up barren,
Barren for all time.
But I dream we'll make a placid home
Denied so far by men,
Become a folk immune
To bigotry and hate,
Devoid of arrogance and desire
For power and domination,
That ambition when it arises
Will be intent for peace instead.

I can only hope,
For my zest for life in youth
Hasn't flickered out with age,
And I beg that men can prove dreams right,
And hope that men will rewrite Man.

THE END

Please use the following pages to write down your thoughts, your inspirations and your solutions to the issues and problems met within the poem, and the poems in the following pages.

Please use the following pages to write down your thoughts, your inspirations and your solutions to the issues and problems met within the poem, and the poems in the following pages.

Please use the following pages to write down your thoughts, your inspirations and your solutions to the issues and problems met within the poem, and the poems in the following pages.

Heaven was a place

Heaven was a place I knew I'd go
Despite the naughty acts of a mischievous boy,
It was assured without a doubt with rooms of toys,
Fields and woods to play, games and ice-cream everyday,
Collecting eggs, frogspawn in jars,
Paddling pools and fishing rods,
No homework to confine, no maths riddles to perplex,
Only crab lines dangling down, sand castles on the beach.

Life was something that would never end,
Death was something you only played:
A Red Indian's arrow, a gangster's bullet,
Diving for cover from mortar shells, and grenades
That killed you dead, then you got up and sped
Off home to buttered bread and strawberry jam,
Collecting crab apples on the way, and berries along with
Green scraped knees, tatty scuffed shoes and far off eyes,
Imagination filled, holding the story of the day.

Old age was for great uncles and great aunts,
Old was something I'd never be, could not conceive,
Yet despite my youthful misperception, and surety in all things,
I acquiesce and bow to Time
That rolls on, indifferent and unforgiving
To the world that is around,
And though Heaven was the place I knew I'd go
It's never seemed so far away,
And the veil that was so thin, at times transparent to my dreaming eye,
Has become a wall, and every bullet fired a brick,
And I fear one more may be the last, and seal us off for good.

Please use the following pages to write down your thoughts, your inspirations and your solutions to the issues and problems met within the poem, and the poems in the following pages.

The ingenuity of dysentery

God, the ingenuity of dysentery
To take a strong, athletic man,
Reduce him to a rake,
Trying to keep stable
On ever shrinking stilts of legs,
Shuffling,
Stumbling towards the head,
His rectum hanging out.

Trousers round his ankles,
Soiled and stinking
Like a babe but worse,
He had no dignity left,
But still it had another trick,
Made him trip as he turned to sit,
Lose his footing, find no grip,
Fall into the hole face first
To swallow his own shit.

Yes, the utter ingenuity,
The complete despicability,
Aided and abetted
By War and its fanatics,
A hapless human ushered
To drown in his own crap.

Please use the following pages to write down your thoughts, your inspirations and your solutions to the issues and problems met within the poem, and the poems in the following pages.

A conscientious objector

There's not much difference between you and I,
We love our country, we're duty bound,
We'd lay down our lives for those we love,
Yet my marching orders and impetus
Originate from a different voice
That asks me to conscientiously object
When you're running off to war,
To stare at prison walls if so desired,
Be tarred and feathered white
Rather than join the merry fight,
Shed blood of father, son
And wholly innocent child,
Lay down another's life
Instead of laying down a gun or knife,
Instead of demanding politicians
Put more faith
In the many manifestations of love,
Be more adept at finding words
That inspire trust instead of fear,
That fight to rouse up ways of peace,
That forbid the picking up of arms,
That believe in peace, instead of war, always,
For ours is to question reasons,
Ours is not to limit questions,
But still we do,
So am I just a fool, to believe
In peace, and only peace?

Please use the following pages to write down your thoughts, your inspirations and your solutions to the issues and problems met within the poem, and the poems in the following pages.

Galipoli

Nobody wished to see
The debacle of Galipoli,
Bodies falling
Emptied of life and blood,
Running into hopeless odds,
But yet they did in thousands,
With armour thick as cloth,
Against well-aimed Turkish guns,
Leaving not much chance, if any,
To meet the end of day,
More probable to rest in sterile soil
Than in a bed of hay.
Yet none turned back, none thought to flee
From Destiny, the path it made -
Rather lose one life
Than lose one's self-respect,
Forsake duty and the soldier's lot -
Such was their courage,
Earning nothing but esteem
From Commonwealth, allies, and enemy alike,
Who won the battle, yet pay homage to the dead
In memory, monuments and history books,
In eulogies carved in stone, in friendship,
To future greet those nations
In peace and gentler ways.

Please use the following pages to write down your thoughts, your inspirations and your solutions to the issues and problems met within the poem, and the poems in the following pages.

My Britain

My Britain is a land of many
Living side by side,
Who believe in peace and tolerance,
Are totally colour blind,
Who look at each and every faith
With moderation and respect,
Who are loyal to the human right
Of each and every man,
That leaves each man at ease
To share this land as a common band
In one common humanity.

I stand beside you willingly

I stand beside you proudly,
With honour I gladly do,
If refusing to be swayed to hatred and contempt
Is how you guide your life,
Never rallying with the ignorant,
Under no banner that defiles,
Holding fast to the sacred middle way,
To peace and acceptance, of others, of their joy.

If your voice is raised in peace, rather than in war
With warmth within your heart,
With purity in your soul,
I repeat it is with honour that
I willingly and steadfastly
Stand closely by your side.

Please use the following pages to write down your thoughts, your inspirations and your solutions to the issues and problems met within the poem, and the poems in the following pages.

Becoming illusion?

When do you decide
When dream becomes illusion,
Who decides the date
When purpose disappears,
When does what you have to do
Transform to what you should have done,
And the monument you thought to build
Empties of achievement,
Mudslides into apathy,
And the rocket that took off so quick
Fails to burst in colour?

When does self-belief and endeavour
Become a waste of time,
When does the journey towards renown
Become too long and steep
And descent more appealing than ascent
When inspiration is abandoned,
Brushed away by doubt?

It's up to you my friend,
The answer lies in how you think:
Will your spirit acquiesce
Or continue yelling out?

Please use the following pages to write down your thoughts, your inspirations and your solutions to the issues and problems met within the poem, and the poems in the following pages.

I heard a sound

I heard a sound I'd never heard,
A baying in the wind,
As Time unleashed upon my trail
And sniffed the air to catch my scent,
Distant yet, upwind, yet closing in
Encouraged by my afternoon nap
And stiff and aching limbs.
The hunt had begun with one outcome,
Only distance covered still unknown:
How wily can I be to ward off Death
Before the finish line?

So catch me if you can,
I'll dodge, backtrack and race,
Your frosty breath may turn hair white,
Your grasping fingers pull it out,
Pluck the tendons at my feet
While steadfastly on my heels.
And when you think I've gone to ground
You'll see there's no-one there,
My lair is empty, light and airy,
As long as cheerful girls with pretty smiles
Keep my heart strings taught and young
I'll dance a merry jig,
Zigzag from your drooling fangs,
And though you'll sink the final bite
The last laugh is on you:
I'll always win and always will
For in one form or another
I'll come back to Earth again.

Please use the following pages to write down your thoughts, your inspirations and your solutions to the issues and problems met within the poem, and the poem on the following page.

The fault beneath the line

Where shall we draw our line today,
Across the sand or across the sea?
Will Kilimanjaro go to the left or to the right,
Shall we add it to the Kaiser's might?
Symmetry is more important,
And aesthetic pleasantness,
So let's go from the 'e' in Acre
And head for the last 'k' in Kirkuk.
Hand me a tissue to sketch a budding thought,
A nation is coming, it's Transjordania's birth,
Let's impose a king from a neighbouring land,
Let's separate and displace,
The people won't resist,
How can they, they don't exist,
And the shining pearl of the north, Lahore,
A toss of a coin will decide,
Will it be Islamic or a Hindi–based mélange?
Hold up the map
And turn it to the light,
Move it this way and that,
Yes, it's a satisfying sight,
Inspect it like a jeweller
Eying over a clear cut edge,
The only thing you will not see
Is the fault beneath the line.

Please use the following pages to write down your thoughts, your inspirations and your solutions to the issues and problems met within the poem, and the poems on the previous pages.